# Enid Blyton

# TOYLAND™ STORIES

## THE GOBLINS AND THE GOOD DEEDS

First published in Great Britain by HarperCollins Publishers Ltd in 1998

1 3 5 7 9 10 8 6 4 2

ISBN: 0 00 136083 3

Cover design and illustrations by County Studio

A CIP catalogue record for this title is available from the British Library.

Printed and bound in Belgium by Proost

# Enid Blyton™

# TOYLAND™ STORIES

## THE GOBLINS AND THE GOOD DEEDS

Collins

*An Imprint of HarperCollinsPublishers*

Sly and Gobbo, the two goblins, were very bored. They wanted to do something bad. But they had done so many bad things over the past few days that they had no ideas left.

"There must be some bad things that we haven't thought of," Gobbo moaned, as they crept out of Dark Wood and tip-toed towards Toy Town.

"Yes, there must be something," said Sly, trying really hard to think. "I know! What about letting down Noddy's tyres?"

"We did that yesterday," Gobbo replied miserably.

Then Sly had another bright idea.

"What about ringing Mr Plod's doorbell and then running away?"

"We did that yesterday as well," grumbled Gobbo. "And the day before. I'm fed up of ringing Mr Plod's doorbell and running away. I want a *new* bad thing to do."

Sly dropped his head. "There isn't anything," he said, letting out a long sigh. "We've done every bad thing there is." Then his face suddenly lifted again, lighting up. "I know!" he exclaimed. "Why don't we do something *good* for a change!"

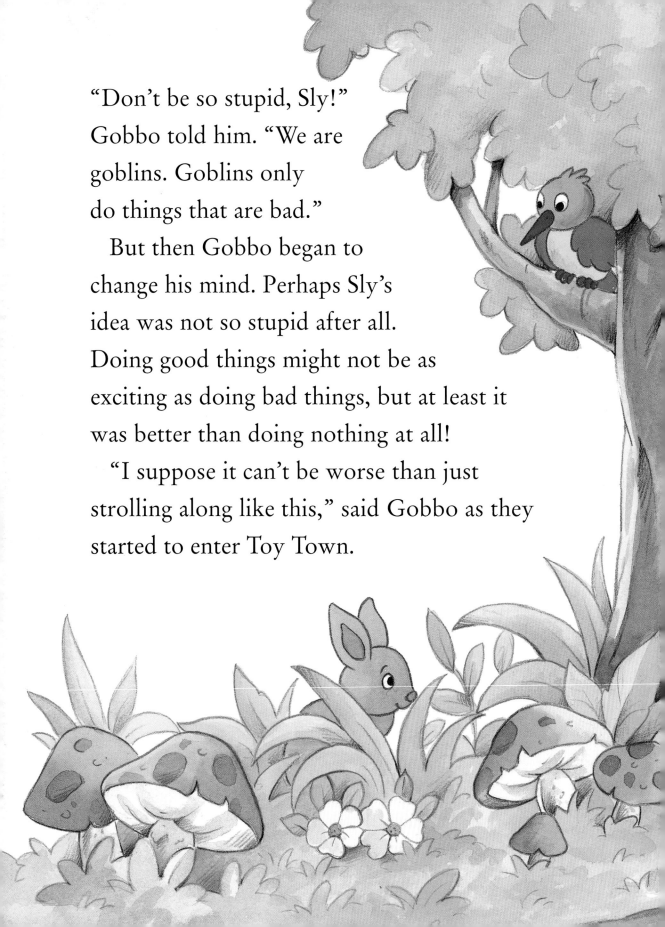

"Don't be so stupid, Sly!" Gobbo told him. "We are goblins. Goblins only do things that are bad."

But then Gobbo began to change his mind. Perhaps Sly's idea was not so stupid after all. Doing good things might not be as exciting as doing bad things, but at least it was better than doing nothing at all!

"I suppose it can't be worse than just strolling along like this," said Gobbo as they started to enter Toy Town.

At that moment Gobbo spotted Milko up ahead.
"Look, there's Milko delivering his milk bottles.
Let's give him a hand."
    This seemed a very *good* thing to do indeed.

Milko looked even more weary delivering his milk than he usually did. His heavy crate forced him to lean right over to one side and he kept groaning as he carried it.

"Let's make it a nice surprise!" Gobbo whispered as they crept up behind the tired milkman. "We'll be as quiet as can be. Then you take one bottle out of his crate and I'll take another!"

So the two goblins crept up behind Milko as softly as they could.

Suddenly Gobbo leapt to the left and Sly to
the right and they each plucked a bottle out
of Milko's crate.

They certainly gave Milko a surprise!
"Here! What are you two bad goblins up to?"
he cried, dropping all the other milk bottles on
to the ground.

The goblins wanted to explain that they had come to help him, but Milko would not give them the chance.

"Help, police!" he wailed. "I've been robbed!" And at that the milkman ran off in search of Mr Plod.

The two goblins shrugged their shoulders at each other. What a strange way to behave when someone was helping you! Still, they were not going to worry about it. The milk bottles they had taken from the crate still had to be delivered.

"There's Miss Pink Cat's house," said Gobbo,
pointing up the road. "She is sure to have milk
delivered. Cats love milk."

"Yes they do, don't they?" Sly grinned. "Let's go
and leave one of these bottles on her doorstep."

They both carried their milk bottles very
carefully. They did not want to drop them.

"Well done, Sly," Gobbo said when they had reached Miss Pink Cat's house. "Now, which bottle shall we leave on the doorstep?"

Gobbo decided that it should be his bottle. He was just bending down, however, when the door suddenly opened. There was Miss Pink Cat. She had come to see if her milk had been delivered.

The two goblins smiled at Miss Pink Cat. She did not smile back.

"About to take my milk from my doorstep, were you?" she cried. Her face was very red and cross. "I'll report you for this!"

Gobbo tried to explain that they were *delivering* her milk, not *taking* it. But when Miss Pink Cat brought out her umbrella, Gobbo decided it best not to try to explain at all.

**"*RUN!*"** he shouted to Sly.

The two goblins only stopped running when
Miss Pink Cat's house was well behind them.
They found themselves outside Noddy's house.
It was then that Sly realised that he was
still carrying his bottle of milk.

"I'm sure Noddy likes milk!" he said brightly.
"I'll just put this bottle on his doorstep."

As Sly was walking towards Noddy's door, however, he suddenly tripped. The bottle of milk flew from his hand and smashed through Noddy's window.

**CRASH!**

Noddy's angry face suddenly appeared.

"So it was you two bad goblins who threw that milk bottle through my window!" he cried. "Just wait until I catch you!"

Sly and Gobbo swapped anxious
glances. It was time to run again. They sped off to
the left, but as they turned the corner they saw Miss
Pink Cat, Milko and Mr Plod running towards them.

They were shaking their fists and Mr Plod kept
blowing his whistle.
**"STOP THIEF!"** they all cried.

The goblins did a quick turnabout but as they
passed Noddy's house again, they saw that
he was jumping into his car.
He was joining the chase as well!

"Back to Dark Wood!" Gobbo cried desperately, running for all he was worth. He frowned as he ran. He could not understand why there were sniggers at his side. "What's so funny, Sly?" he gasped crossly.

"Just all this!" Sly panted, moving his legs as fast as they would go. "Being good isn't so boring after all. In fact, it's just as exciting as being bad!"

# THE NODDY CLASSIC LIBRARY
## by Enid Blyton™

Available in hardback
Published by HarperCollins